Tales from the Bamboo Grove

Tales from the Bamboo Grove

by Yoko Kawashima Watkins

Illustrations by
Jean and Mou-sien Tseng

Simon & Schuster Books for Young Readers

SIMON & SCHUSTER BOOKS FOR YOUNG READERS
An imprint of Simon & Schuster Children's Publishing Division
1230 Avenue of the Americas
New York, New York 10020
First edition
Printed and bound in the United States of America

10 9 8 7 6 5 4 3 2
The text of this book is set in 15 point Berkley O.S. Book.
Typography by Cathy Bobak

Library of Congress Cataloging-in-Publication Data
Watkins, Yoko Kawashima.
Tales from the bamboo grove / by Yoko Kawashima Watkins.—1st ed.
p.   cm.
Summary: A collection of Japanese folktales
recalled from the author's childhood.
ISBN 0-02-792525-0
[1. Folklore—Japan.]   I. Title.
PZ8.1.W336Tal   1992
398.2'0952—dc20   91-38218

·ABOUT THE ARTWORK

The calligraphy in the panel facing the title page
is Japanese for *Tales from the Bamboo Grove*.
Similarly, each separate story title is included in its
accompanying illustration. This calligraphy is by
Yoko Kawashima Watkins. Enclosed in the circle that appears
on each illustration is the artists' chop, one Chinese character for
their last name, Tseng. The chop is the traditional way
that Chinese and Japanese artists sign their illustrations.
The pictures were done with brush and ink on Bristol board.

For my children,
Donnie, Ronnie, John, and Michelle . . .

and to Barbara Lalicki,
who led me to reminisce about my childhood's happy hours,
my sincere gratitude

Contents

Contents

Tales from the Bamboo Grove

Introduction

UNTIL I WAS ELEVEN AND A HALF I LIVED IN NANAM, NORTH Korea, where winter came early and spring came slow. Our cozy house stood by a tall and graceful bamboo grove, where I frolicked.

During suppertime it was the Kawashima family's custom to gather in a twelve tatami-mat room* and eat from individual vermilion-lacquered trays. Father sat in front of the tokonoma,† with my brother, Hideyo, on his left. If male

*Each tatami mat is three by six feet, two inches thick, and made of sweet-smelling straw.
†An alcove that is simply decorated with a long, hanging scroll-painting. Flower arrangements sit beneath the scroll.

guests were present they would take their places next to Hideyo. My sister, Ko, and I sat on Father's right. Lady guests or my girlfriends usually sat next to me. Mother always sat at the end to serve us.

It was Father's habit to listen to whatever his children had to say. If our friends were present, Father would listen to them also. So our suppertime would last for two to three hours. No matter what concerned us, we told Father. He listened to each of us carefully, delighted and sometimes serious, before giving us his opinions. After these conversations Father would say, "It's my turn to talk! Be comfortable!" Then I'd hurry to sit on his lap, ready for story time.

He told us folktales from the villages in northern Japan where he and Mother were born. If the story was divided into two parts, I could not wait for the next evening, when Mother would finish Father's story. My parents' faces were bright whenever they told us the tales that had been passed on to them by their ancestors. How little I knew that telling us these folktales comforted my parents, who lived so far away from their homeland villages. When telling us the stories, they must have reminisced about bygone days precious to their hearts. Sometimes they would sing folk songs and urge us to clap our hands and sing along. If I was sick they would sit by my futon and tell me stories to make me smile. Often, my parents' guests told us their regional folktales, which pleased us, especially the one Corporal Matsumura told called "Why Is Seawater Salty?" Telling this tale was his way of thanking Ko and me for visiting him at the army hospital when he was straying between life and death.

When I had the measles, I said to Mother, "My face is breaking out and I look ugly." As Mother sat by me, playing with my hands, she told me "Dragon Princess, Tatsuko." When she finished the story, I asked her if she would like to have a beautiful girl forever. She shook her head. "I would rather have a daughter who is healthy enough to frolic outside!" A few days later, Mother told me "The Fox Wife." She explained that between A.D. 1400–1550 farmers suffered deeply because the landowners had placed a heavy rice tax on them. Farmers who protested against the tax were killed. It was a farmer's dream to have a better life, but speaking out was dangerous. To make themselves feel better, the farmers made up a story, "The Fox Wife."

Yaeko was in my class. She was taller and stronger than I. Her father was a fishmonger. Though they were poor, she came to school in clean and neatly mended clothes. But her mother became ill after giving birth to a baby boy, and she could not care for the family. Yaeko stopped coming to school and looked after her mother and baby brother. One day on my way home from the school, I saw Yaeko carrying her baby brother on her back, kneeling down by the river and doing laundry. I ran to her. The baby was screaming. Yaeko said her mother didn't have enough milk for the baby. "If mother was well, everything would be all right," sniffled Yaeko, wiping her tears on her sleeves, which were dirty and poorly mended. That evening, I told my family about Yaeko. Then Ko told us "Yayoi and the Spirit Tree," and ended, "I trust Yaeko will be rewarded someday." Ko said she learned the story from a new girl in school who had moved to Nanam from southern Japan.

There was a bully in my class at school. Father was away on the evening that I told the family about him as I ate. "Everyone in my class is troubled by him," I concluded. Hideyo smiled and said, "There is always someone stronger than the bully." Then he introduced us to the story "Monkey and Crab."

The shadows of World War II darkened Father's heart. Still, at suppertime he was smiling as he listened to what we had to say. We spoke of the war. Father was very calm and told us "The Grandmother Who Became an Island." Soon he had to leave for Manchuria to attend an important meeting. It was the last folktale I heard from Father. I did not see him for another six years.

Reminiscing recently, Ko and I realized that these folktales not only delighted us when we were children, they also taught us the importance of history, love, wisdom, morals, and peace.

—YOKO KAWASHIMA WATKINS

Dragon Princess, Tatsuko

Long, long ago, in a small village in northern Japan, lived a most beautiful girl called Tatsuko. She lived with her mother and worked hard to help her. The girl and her mother were poor, but they enjoyed each day.

In spring Tatsuko would join the young people of the village to clear the fields and burn the weeds. The glow of the fire tinted the maidens' faces with gold. Among them, Tatsuko, with her lively black eyes and soft pink lips, was most exquisite.

In summer the maidens would gather hemp. At night they would cook the hemp in a huge iron kettle that belonged to the village, so that it could be woven when it was dry. While working, Tatsuko sang in the gentle summer wind. Her silver bell-like voice carried over the entire village. All the villagers stopped what they were doing and gathered around. Just to see Tatsuko and hear her sing soothed their tired, aching muscles.

When autumn came, the maidens would cut hay to feed the horses. The horses were happy to have fresh hay, and they neighed for joy. Tatsuko's heart was filled with gladness by the healthy horses. Choosing one, she would hop upon its back and gallop among the tall grasses.

When winter came, Tatsuko would sit by the *irori*, a fireplace set in the wooden floor, making straw shoes. Sometimes she would chase wild rabbits in the snow-covered field, and when she caught them she would make winter soup. From the fur, she made warm vests to sell at the city market. During the long winter months, she dyed and wove hemp into kimono material, working by candlelight.

Tatsuko's mother was proud of her daughter, and everyone was proud that the beautiful girl belonged to their village. However, Tatsuko was not aware of her beauty. She never thought of what it meant to be beautiful. She lived each day joyfully.

Late one autumn she was in the mountains, picking chestnuts and mushrooms. Tired, she decided to rest. When Tatsuko knelt down to drink some water from the pond, she saw herself on the surface of the water and noticed that her hair was all tangled. While she combed her hair she rested and watched her reflection in the water. "How beautiful . . ." she said to herself. "Am I as beautiful as this?" She gazed at her reflection on the water's surface.

From that day on she was changed. Instead of riding horses or working in the fields, she sat deep in thought. In winter she would not chase the wild rabbits. She only sat by the irori, gazing at the flames, thinking.

"Soon spring comes and then summer and autumn . . . and then again winter. Thus everyone grows old," thought Tatsuko. "Beautiful maidens are no exception. From

辰子姫物語

hard work year after year a maiden's back bends in half, and her long black hair turns to gray. Ah, am I too growing old? I cannot stand to imagine myself an old woman!"

Tatsuko's chest tightened to think that time was passing. She began to curse herself for being born. She could not sleep at night. "How I want to stay young and beautiful!" She turned and tossed in her bed.

One night she suddenly got up and said to herself, "I am going to the shrine and pray." Quietly she left the house. There was still snow on the ground, and it was cold in the moonlight. But Tatsuko walked to the shrine on the mountain path, where she prayed. "Merciful God! Please let me stay beautiful forever. I do not wish to grow old!"

In storm, in wind, night after night, Tatsuko went to the shrine to pray. She often heard the eerie sounds of nearby animals. She was frightened when tree branches fell. She would hear the sad cry of an owl. There were times when she was soaked by rain and times when she was lost. Still she kept on. She grew thin, but her face increased in beauty. Her black, black eyes began to shine mysteriously.

A hundred days and nights passed in this way. Then, as she sat in front of the shrine, Tatsuko heard a voice from above. "Tatsuko! Poor Tatsuko! If you really want to stay beautiful forever, listen. You will find a spring north of here. Drink that water. But I warn you, before taking the drink, you must think once more. After you drink you will not be permitted to take back your wish. If you have regrets later on, it will be too late."

"If I can keep my beauty forever, I will never, never regret!" answered the girl.

A few days later, Tatsuko and three other maidens went to the mountain to gather branches for firewood. Tatsuko secretly thought, "Today I will drink the spring water." The maidens gathered branches and bound them together all morning. By afternoon the other maidens were tired. As soon as they fell asleep, Tatsuko stealthily took off, heading north into the deep forest.

The forest was filled with the fragrance of wildflowers. Tatsuko was ecstatic. Soon she would be beautiful forever! Her anticipation grew, and she hastened her steps. She saw a spring gushing out among the huge rocks. "The spring!" she shouted. She flattened herself on the ground and began to drink the ice-cold water. Even when she was no longer thirsty, even when she was full, she kept on drinking. Gradually Tatsuko came to feel a strong heat inside her body. She tried to stand up, but felt dizzy, for right in front of her eyes there was a vast fire. She fainted.

The three maidens awoke from their nap. Tatsuko was gone. They thought she was still gathering branches and they kept calling her name as they searched through the forest.

In the distance they heard Tatsuko's voice faintly. So they ran toward the sound. To the spring. There, coiled and lifting its head, was a fierce dragon! "Oh, no!" shouted the three maidens. As they ran back to the village, the entire earth darkened, thunder roared, and it stormed.

"What? Tatsuko a dragon? You are crazy!" shouted Tatsuko's mother. But the news quickly spread through the entire village.

The maidens were trembling and could not stop. The villagers, seeing the mountain spit fire and feeling the earth shake, thought they heard the truth.

"Oh, my Tatsuko! My Tatsuko!" screamed the mother. She ran to the mountain and to the spring. All the villagers followed. The mountain was not their familiar mountain anymore. There were no trees, only the sound of waves. "Strange!" the mother and villagers thought. The waves came closer and closer. Soon, in front of their eyes, a gigantic lake appeared.

"Tatsuko! Tatsuko!" the mother called. But the lake was silent. "Tatsuko!" the mother screamed in desperation.

Then the mother and the villagers saw a huge spray of water in the center of the lake. As the spray came nearer, a gigantic rainbow surrounded it. Out came the dragon, whose scales were gleaming with rainbow color. The mother was frightened and shouted, "My beautiful Tatsuko! My daughter Tatsuko is not a dragon!"

The dragon disappeared into the lake, but when it came up again with a huge spray it stood in front of the mother as the most beautiful Tatsuko. The mother cried, "Oh, Tatsuko, let us go home! Quickly, let us go home!"

Tatsuko silently shook her head. "Honorable Mother, do forgive me. I am not human anymore. I prayed never to grow old. Now I am the dragon you just saw, the goddess of this lake."

Tatsuko's mother was crying out loud. "I do not like you to become the goddess of the lake or a dragon. I want you to be my daughter, my human daughter! Now let's go home."

"Please do not be sad, Mother. If you are sad, I too am sad. I know you love to eat fish. As long as you live I shall give you fresh fish. Whenever you eat them, do think of your daughter, forever beautiful and young. Good-bye, my beloved mother. Stay well!"

As soon as she bid farewell to her mother, Tatsuko changed back into the dragon and swam deep into the lake.

"Tatsuko! Tatsuko!" screamed her mother. But there was only the sound of waves hitting the shore. The mother was weeping. Suddenly her tears changed into beautiful fish and jumped into the lake after the dragon.

The Fox Wife

LONG AGO, A KIND YOUNG MAN CALLED SHINKICHI LIVED IN A
shack. He was very poor and his only farm tool was the
hoe. Though he worked hard in his small rice field day after
day, his life never became better. He wanted to marry a
pretty maiden from his village, but it was only a dream.

One extremely hot summer day, a beautiful maiden in
traveling clothes was out walking. As always, Shinkichi was
in his field working. When the maiden was about to pass
by him, she fainted.

15

Shinkichi ran to help her. He put his hand on her forehead. She was burning with fever, and she was panting.

"She is going to die if I do not do something," thought Shinkichi. He carried her on his back and hurried home. He wanted to put her on a bed, but he had no bed. So he gathered weeds, shaped them carefully, covered them with his thin kimono, and laid her down.

Every day and every night he nursed her. Gradually the maiden regained consciousness. When she was able to get up from the homemade bed, she was completely well.

"I am deeply grateful for your care," said the maiden, bowing her head to Shinkichi. "I do not know how to repay you. So if you will allow me to stay for a while and help you in the field or with household chores, I will be happy."

Shinkichi said, "You are too frail to be working in the field." Then he asked her name. He asked about her family, and where she was heading when she fainted on that hot summer day. She said she could not reveal her name. She had lived deep in the mountains with her parents and brothers, but a pack of wolves had killed them. She said she'd

16

been heading to a village where she could be safe from the wild beasts.

"If you do not mind, I want to stay here and become your servant," said the maiden.

Shinkichi was glad to accept her offer, as he could not work all day in the field and still do his laundry at the river, and he certainly could not mend his clothes.

The maiden was hardworking and gentle-hearted. Every young man in the village envied Shinkichi. And that autumn, after the harvest, Shinkichi and the maiden became husband and wife. The married couple worked hard, and their lives became better than before. Young men in the village envied Shinkichi all the more.

After two years, Shinkichi and his wife were blessed with a baby boy, who was just as beautiful as his mother. They named the baby Morime.

But one day, this beautiful Morime became ill. The couple nursed their son day and night, praying for his recovery.

Shinkichi neglected his field to care for his son. Everyone in the village had begun planting rice, but Shinkichi's field was not even prepared for planting when the boy finally became well. Now Shinkichi worked until he was so tired that he could not even see an inch in front of him. When everyone in his village had finished planting, Shinkichi was finally ready to plant his first rice seedling. He was worried about how he would accomplish this important task. If he did not finish planting soon, the harvest would not mature, and he could not pay the rice tax. He feared the landowner would take away his field if he could not pay the rice tax. But he did not tell his wife of his worries. He did not want to burden her.

One morning on his way to the rice field, Shinkichi was worrying about how he would finish planting by the next evening. But when he came to the field, lo! His rice field had been planted. As he looked at his field closely, he was even more surprised. The rice seedlings had been planted upside down! "What is this?" shouted Shinkichi.

He ran to his home and called, "My dear wife . . . my dear wife . . . great surprise! Someone planted the rice seedlings for us!"

"That is splendid!" Shinkichi's wife was holding sweet Morime and smiling.

"But you see, the seedlings are all planted upside down!" said Shinkichi.

Suddenly the wife's face turned pale. She handed Morime to her husband and leaped toward the field. She ran, leaping faster than the forest beasts. As she kept leaping, she turned into a long, bushy-tailed white fox. Shinkichi was taken aback. "My wife is a white fox!" he murmured.

The Fox Wife arrived at her husband's rice field and loudly sang a strange song:

> *Ah, be merciful, do feed my son,*
> *When the inspectors come to check the field,*
> *Show them a poor yield of rice. . . .*

Still holding his son as Fox Wife sang, Shinkichi saw all the upside-down rice seedlings turn right-side up. The Fox Wife ran close and spoke very sadly to her husband. "Please forgive me. I cannot live with you and our son anymore.

Please take good care of our Morime. . . . I beg you!" Then she took a giant leap and disappeared.

Autumn arrived. As they did every year, the government inspectors went around and checked the village rice fields to set the rice tax. A thriving field cost a farmer a heavy sum. There was no thriving rice on Shinkichi's field, and yet, as soon as the inspectors left the rice plants grew and grew.

"Oh, I see," said Shinkichi, "why my Fox Wife was singing that strange song. I understand what it meant now." Then he hummed to Morime,

Ah, be merciful, do feed my son,
When the inspectors come to check the field,
Show them a poor yield of rice. . . .

Why Is Seawater Salty?

LONG AGO, TWO BROTHERS LIVED IN TAOI VILLAGE. THEIR PARents had died in a terrible storm while fishing. Now, when the weather was good, the brothers went to sea to catch fish to sell at the village market.

The elder brother wanted to keep their earnings all to himself, and he secretly wished that his younger brother would get out of the house. So the elder brother made up a sad story and told everyone. He said that in spite of all his hard work, he could not take care of his younger brother anymore. Then he threw his younger brother out of the house. "Now the house and the earnings are all mine! I will be rich, I will be rich!" The elder brother grinned.

By and by, Younger Brother got married. He and his bride rented a small piece of land and farmed. They lived in a corner of the animal shed. They were very poor, but happy in love. However, when winter came, there was no work. The fields were frozen, and they could not go to sea to catch fish, because the wind was high and the waves were angry. New Year's Eve came, but there was not a grain of rice left in their rice bin. So Younger Brother went to his elder brother's house and, bowing his head deeply, begged, "Please loan us five cups of rice for the New Year's celebration."

"What?" shouted the elder brother. "You don't have the rice to celebrate New Year's Eve? You should not have gotten married. Now you have two mouths to feed! Stupid! Go beg somewhere else!" He chased his younger brother away. Younger Brother could not go home to his wife empty-handed. With his head hung low, he wandered toward the mountain.

When he came to the mountain pass, he saw a feeble old man with a long white beard gathering branches. Younger Brother helped gather branches and bound them together for the old man.

"Thank you, young man," said the old man. He asked, "Where are you going?"

"Tonight is New Year's Eve, but I have no rice to offer to our god or to celebrate with my wife. I thought I might find something on the mountain."

"How sad," said the old man. "Because you helped me, I will give you this." He handed Younger Brother a large wheat cake. The old man continued, "Take this cake and go to the shrine over there. There is a cave behind the shrine. Walk along inside the cave until you meet the Little People. They will see your wheat cake and beg for it, and they will offer you gold or silver. But you must say, 'I will exchange this wheat cake with you, not for gold or silver but for your Stone Hand Mill.' Do you understand?"

The younger brother nodded and thanked the old man before going into the cave. Sure enough, after a time, he saw many Little People gathered about. They were making such a commotion! Some of them were trying to gather beautiful wild lilies for their dwelling, but they could not even pull the lilies out of the ground. They were stumbling over the flowers. It was a funny sight.

Younger Brother burst out laughing and said, "Well, let me help you gather the flowers for your house!"

"Wow! You are a giant! How powerful!" exclaimed the Little People when they saw Younger Brother. Then they saw the wheat cake.

"You are carrying something unusual. Give it to us," said the Little People.

"I don't think I will," answered Younger Brother. "This is my important wheat cake. I will only give it to you if you give me your Stone Hand Mill."

"That would be trouble. The Stone Hand Mill is our treasure. You cannot find another one in this world. We shall give you gold." They offered many pieces of gold to Younger Brother.

"Sorry!" said Younger Brother. "I don't need gold. I can

only exchange my wheat cake for your Stone Hand Mill."
So the Little People gave in. They brought out the Stone
Hand Mill and exchanged it for the wheat cake.

When Younger Brother came back to the mountain pass,
the old man was waiting for him. He instructed Younger
Brother, "Now you have the Mill. Turn the handle to the
right, and keep on turning. Whatever you wish for will
appear. If you wish to stop it, then turn the handle to the
left." Younger Brother was overjoyed and, after thanking the
old man many times, went home.

"Where were you all this time?" asked his wife, worrying.
"Did your elder brother loan you some rice?"

"No, but bring a straw mat, and watch." Smiling, Younger
Brother put the Stone Hand Mill down on the straw mat.
He did exactly what the old man told him to do, saying
"Rice . . . Rice . . ." and turning the handle to the right. Out
came so much rice that it made a small mountain in front
of the wife. When he turned the handle to the left, the rice
stopped. The wife could not believe her eyes.

Younger Brother turned the Mill handle to the right and

wished, "Salmon . . . Salmon . . ." Out popped fresh salmon.

"Now we are rich. We do not have to live in this shed anymore," said Younger Brother. He turned the handle to the right and wished, "A new house and two horses!" There stood a lovely new house and a stable with two horses inside. Younger Brother and his wife produced many things to sell in the village and at the faraway town market. They also shared their good fortune with the poor. Now everyone in the village was happy and comfortable.

When the elder brother heard about Younger Brother's fortune, he had to see it for himself. He stealthily went to his brother's house. Peering through the window, he saw Younger Brother turning the handle to produce rice cakes and candies for the village children to use for their Girls' Day celebration. "It is the magic Stone Hand Mill!" thought the elder brother. "I want it!"

That night when everyone was asleep, the elder brother went to Younger Brother's house and stole the Stone Hand Mill, along with the candies and rice cakes. He ran to the beach, hopped into his fishing boat, and grinned. "Goody,

海の水はなぜ辛い

弐弖

goody! I will sail away, and I will be enormously rich!"

He would not give things to others, as Younger Brother had done!

As he rowed his boat through the waves, he became hungry. So he ate the stolen candies and rice cakes. Because all that he ate was sweet, he wanted something salty.

In those days there was no salt in seawater. Salt was taken from the mountain plants. It was so expensive that the poor could not afford it. Because the elder brother wanted to eat something salty, he turned the handle of the Stone Hand Mill to the right and ordered, "Salt come out!" The salt came out. It soon filled the boat. The elder brother shouted, "Stop! Stop!" But the salt kept on coming, and the boat began to sink. "What am I going to do? What am I going to do?" he cried. He knew nothing of how to stop the Mill.

The boat sank, along with the elder brother.

Because no one ever went deep down into the sea to turn the Stone Hand Mill's handle to the left, even to this day it keeps turning, turning, and pouring salt into the ocean.

That's why seawater is salty!

Yayoi and the Spirit Tree

LONG AGO, A WEALTHY MAN'S HOUSE STOOD ON ONE SIDE OF a hill. On the other side of the hill lived a humble family, an ailing mother and her daughter, Yayoi. On top of the hill stood a Tall Tree that almost reached the clouds. Early every morning Yayoi would pass in front of the Tall Tree on her way to work. She was a servant in the wealthy man's household. Late every night she would pass the Tall Tree on her way back home to help her sick mother.

Whenever she was sad or tired, she would lean on the Tall Tree and speak to it as a friend. Every time she spoke, the branches on the tree swayed, as if the tree understood her.

Before Yayoi left work she was fed at the wealthy man's house. But she ate only a little and saved the rest for her mother. Often she would run past the tree on the dark hill road. She'd rush into her house calling, "Mother, I am home. I have brought you something good to eat."

One night Yayoi was hurrying home, carrying her mother's supper in a small wooden box. Yayoi was happy to think that in three more days her three-year contract with the wealthy man would be over. When she came to the top of the hill, suddenly the sky darkened, and it poured. "Ah! Mother's supper will be wet!" she said, running under the Tall Tree.

"Tall Tree," said Yayoi, "in just three more days I will no longer be a servant. I will be able to stay with Mother! Thank you for listening to my troubles all these years."

"Miss Yayoi! Miss Yayoi!" someone called. Yayoi was surprised and looked around. There was absolutely no one out in the storm. Again she heard someone calling her name. "Miss Yayoi!"

"Who is calling me?"

"I am the Spirit of the Tree. For the past three years I have watched you go to and from work faithfully. You are commendable!" Then the Spirit of the Tree said, "I am going to tell you something wonderful."

Yayoi was surprised that the Tall Tree had spoken, and she could hardly breathe for listening to what the Spirit of the Tree had to say.

"In three days the lord's woodcutters will come and cut me from my roots. They are going to take me near water and make me into the lord's ship. When the ship is ready to launch, I will not go forward. There will be thousands of people who will pull and push, trying to launch me, but no one will be able to move me. The lord will exclaim, 'Anyone who can launch the ship will be given whatever he desires for the rest of his life!' Then you will go by the ship's bow and sing in a lullaby tune, 'This is Yayoi, launch! This is Yayoi, launch!' Soon the ship will launch and float on the water." Then the voice disappeared. The storm stopped, and the sky began to clear. Yayoi went home bewildered. "The Tall Tree cannot speak," she thought.

"Mother, Mother, I am sorry I was late this evening," called Yayoi as she entered her humble home. "When it rained, I had to stay under the Tall Tree for a while." But she did not tell her mother what the Spirit of the Tree had told her.

The next morning early, Yayoi passed in front of the Tall Tree. She stopped a few moments and bowed, for she had no time to speak. Last night's sudden rain had refreshed the tree. The leaves had darkened to a richer green, and the branches had stretched up even more!

On the third day, Yayoi's contract was fulfilled. She did not have to work again for the wealthy man. She was free and starting home when she heard noise in the distance. Hundreds of woodcutters were striking at the Tall Tree.

"Ah! What I heard the other night was true. I heard the

Spirit of the Tree!" thought Yayoi. She hurried to her humble home, where her mother waited.

Every day Yayoi took her mother for a walk to the top of the mountain. From there they could see the Tall Tree in the distance, way down by the water, gradually changing into the shape of a ship. Yayoi felt sad about losing her friend.

Six months passed. The ship was completed. It was a gorgeous ship, the greatest ship people had ever seen on the earth. The gallant lord came, followed by thousands of his mighty warriors.

"Well then, let us launch this splendid ship!" yelled the lord in delight.

But the ship would not launch. The shipbuilders, wood-cutters, and the lord's warriors all pulled and pushed but the ship would not budge. The lord became irritated and shouted, "Whoever launches this ship will be rewarded for the rest of his life!" But no one was able to do it.

Yayoi stepped forward and said to the lord in a faint voice, "I think I can launch the ship."

"What? You? Feeble-looking maiden?" said the lord. "Don't joke." Everyone roared in laughter. But the lord was desperate to launch the ship, so he said, "Try it! If you are fooling me, I will slash you to pieces!"

Yayoi went to the ship. She gently touched the bow and sang in a lullaby tune, "This is Yayoi, launch! This is Yayoi, launch!" Slowly, slowly the ship began to slide into the sea. It floated on the water majestically.

"You are the most powerful young maiden I've ever seen!" marveled the lord.

"Indeed not. I am just a plain maiden, Yayoi."

"As I promised, you shall be rewarded with whatever you wish for," said the lord.

"I do not wish a thing for myself. But I would like to have enough food and warm clothing for my beloved mother, and I want her to see a doctor."

With this care the mother regained her health, and Yayoi and her mother lived peacefully ever after.

Monkey and Crab

One fine day mother crab took her two children for a walk in the mountains. She found a rice ball. "This will be our supper," said Mother Crab. Walking along, they met Monkey, who was holding a persimmon seed. When Monkey saw the rice ball, he wanted it so very badly.

"Mrs. Crab," called Monkey. "The persimmon seed is better than a rice ball."

"Why?" asked Mother Crab.

"When you and your children eat a rice ball, there is no more," said Monkey, "but if you plant this persimmon seed, it will grow and bear plenty of fruit. You will never go hungry. If you would like to have this seed, I'll be glad to exchange it for your rice ball."

Mother Crab thought, "If the seed bears juicy and sweet fruit, my children will be very happy." So she exchanged the rice ball for the persimmon seed.

Monkey devoured the rice ball at once.

Mother Crab and her children tilled their garden and buried the seed. Every day they watered the ground and spoke to the seed. "Hurry and shoot out! Otherwise we will snip you with our claws!" The persimmon seed did not like the idea of being snipped, so it quickly sprouted.

The happy Crab family weeded around the young tree, fertilized it, and sang, "Hurry and grow! Hurry and bear plenty of fruit! Otherwise we will snip you with our claws!"

Soon the young tree became tall, and it blossomed. The blossoms became beautiful green persimmons. Every day the Crab family looked up at the fruit and sang, "Hurry and ripen! Hurry and ripen!" Finally, when autumn came, the persimmons ripened bright red, and the Crab family was overjoyed. "Let us harvest!" exclaimed the Crab children. But the tree was so tall that they could not reach the fruit, even when they brought their ladder.

When Monkey saw the ripe, red persimmons from the mountaintop, he came to call on the Crab family. "Indeed splendid!" marveled Monkey. He saw that the Crabs could not reach the persimmons, so he offered to get the harvest for them.

"Thank you, you are very kind," said Mother Crab.

"I will drop each fruit down to you carefully," said Monkey as he climbed up the tree. But when he sat on the branch, he chose the ripest ones and began eating them and smacking his lips. "Most delicious! Delicious!"

Beneath the tree, Mother Crab and her children were waiting for Monkey to drop the fruit. "Please, Mr. Monkey! Drop us some," called the Crab children. "We want to taste them."

Monkey grabbed several green persimmons and yelled,

"Eat these!" He threw them at the Crabs. One of them hit Mother Crab's back and she fainted. The Crab children tried to help their mother, but she was still. The children began crying aloud. When Mr. Mortar heard the cry of the little Crabs, he hurried over to them.

From the tree, Monkey saw huge, wooden Mr. Mortar coming. He is huge so that he can pound cooked rice into rice cakes for the New Year's festival. Monkey was afraid of being crushed by Mr. Mortar. So he crammed the rest of the ripe fruit into a basket and quickly ran away to his house on the mountaintop.

Mr. Mortar heard all about the slyness of Monkey as he made a stretcher for Mrs. Crab. Carefully, carefully, he and the Crab children brought Mother Crab home. They bandaged her head and back.

"Such a sly, wicked monkey! He ate the rice ball and the persimmons. On top of that he injured Mrs. Crab! We must punish him!" thought Mr. Mortar. So he wrote letters to Mr. Bee and Mr. Chestnut, asking them to meet him at the Crabs' house. Soon Mr. Bee and Mr. Chestnut arrived. They all had a meeting to decide how to teach Monkey a lesson.

When they set out for Monkey's house on the top of the mountain, the Crab children went with them. On the way to Monkey's house was a steep cliff. Everyone but heavy Mr. Mortar was able to climb it easily. Mr. Bee, Mr. Chestnut, and the Crab children had to pull Mr. Mortar up the cliff with a long rope. Finally they came near Monkey's house. Mr. Bee flew and investigated. Monkey was not at home.

"I will be hiding in the fireplace," said Mr. Chestnut.

"I will be hiding by the water jar," said Mr. Bee.

The Crab children crawled under the porch. Mr. Mortar went up on the roof.

They all waited for Monkey's return.

Monkey came strutting home, feeling good and proud of how he'd spent his day tricking, stealing, and hurting every-one! "It certainly was a super time!" Monkey smiled. "I am thirsty. I'll have a cup of tea." He sat by the fireplace and built a fire for the hot water. When the fire was good and hot, out popped well-roasted Mr. Chestnut. He landed on Monkey's forehead.

"Ouch, hot! Ouch, hot!" cried Monkey. He ran to the water jar to put water on his forehead. But waiting Mr. Bee stung Monkey everywhere!

"Hurt! Hurt! I can't see! I can't see!" screamed Monkey, trying to run away from home. Then huge, wooden Mr. Mortar dropped on Monkey. Monkey was crushed and could not move. Out came the Crab children, and they began to pinch Monkey's arms, legs, cheeks, and even his nose.

"Everybody was a victim of your slyness," said Mr. Mortar. "Do you realize how bad you have been?" Monkey could hardly breathe. He'd been crushed, pinched, burnt, and stung. He was aching.

"I was bad! Forgive me," cried Monkey. "Please, please forgive me."

"You must ask Mrs. Crab for forgiveness," replied Mr. Mortar.

"I will! I will!" whined Monkey.

So everybody brought Monkey back to Mrs. Crab's home. She was awake but still very weak.

"I will never do bad things anymore." Monkey apologized,

bowing his head deeply. "Please forgive me. I will do my penance."

"Firmly promise?" asked Mother Crab. When he said "Yes," she forgave him. She said to her children, "Make tea and let us have some. Tea of Peace."

Monkey kept his word. He became good, and the entire community lived happily ever after.

The Grandmother
Who Became an Island

LONG AGO, IN THE LOWER PART OF HOKKAIDO, THERE WAS A war between two Ainu tribes. The chief of one tribe, Ekashi, was a gallant and brave man. But during a surprise attack on his village, he was killed. Still, the enemy chief's mind was not at ease.

He knew that Ekashi's son, Tonkuru, had run away with his grandmother. "They are somewhere, still alive," the enemy chief thought. "Until they are both dead I cannot sleep in peace." So he sent his warriors to the woods.

島になったお婆さん

Little Tonkuru was being pulled along by his grand-mother, who was running and pushing through the deep forest. Soon they came upon an open field, and suddenly the enemy's warriors yelled, "There they are!"

"Tonkuru! Come this way," exclaimed the grandmother. Holding her grandson's hand as tightly as possible, she ran back into the forest. In the forest they heard the enemy voices. "Tonkuru! Come out! You are surrounded!"

"Ah, Tonkuru! Let us flee a different way!" The grand-mother ran to the west, and to the east . . . but she was not holding Tonkuru's hand. He was not with her. She still felt the warmth of Tonkuru's little hand in hers as she sat on the ground and wept. "Just when did we separate?" she wondered. She could not call the boy's name out loud for fear the enemy would find her and capture Tonkuru. She called Tonkuru's name in her heart as she searched for him in the dark forest.

The sun went down. But the grandmother kept searching for Tonkuru, behind huge trees and in the caves. She thought, "He is hiding in the deep weeds," and she looked for him there. But no Tonkuru. Soon she came to Lake Kucharo. The surface of the lake was calm in the moonlight.

"Oh, Kucharo, god of the lake, have you seen my grandson?" asked the grandmother. Kucharo did not answer. "You mean he has not passed by here?" Again the grandmother wept. Then she asked, "Kucharo, please let me stay here overnight. . . . I am so tired, and I cannot walk anymore." But the god of the lake did not answer.

The grandmother pulled all her energy together.

She walked until she saw another lake. It was Lake Shuma, and nearby stood majestic Shuma Mountain. Lake Shuma was much colder than Lake Kucharo and appeared overpoweringly large. The mountain looked fierce. The grandmother was frightened, but with trembling voice she begged to the god of the mountain. "Please, Kamuinupuri, I beg you, allow me to rest by the lake."

Kamuinupuri said most gently, "Fine, fine. You may rest as long as your heart desires."

The grandmother felt at ease and lay down on the grass. As she stretched out her arms and legs, she felt at peace.

But then she thought about Tonkuru. She cried and prayed that he was well somewhere.

"Oh why, oh why do human beings attack and kill each other? I do not want to be a human anymore." She gazed at the lake.

"I would like to be an island. If I become an island, someday my grandson Tonkuru will come to visit me. If he is alive."

She knelt and petitioned the god of the mountain, Kamuinupuri, and the god of Lake Shuma. "Please turn me into an island and let me stay here."

So the grandmother became an island. The most beautiful island on the lake. Here birds sing their love songs and nest in the thick woods. Fruit trees thrive in all seasons, and salmon and trout play tag around the island. The grandmother continues to wait for Tonkuru's coming.

Even now, when someone visits the island by boat, the grandmother thinks Tonkuru has finally come, but her cry of joy turns to rain on clear summer days and to snow in winter.

YOKO KAWASHIMA WATKINS spent many of her childhood years in northeastern Korea, where her father worked as a Japanese government official. In 1945, during World War II, the threat of a military attack forced her to flee Korea for Japan with her mother and older sister, Ko.

The author's life as a refugee is told in her ALA Notable Book, *So Far from the Bamboo Grove.*

After the war, Yoko Kawashima Watkins began working as a translator at a U.S. Air Force base in Japan, where she met her husband, Donald. Today the Watkinses live in Brewster, Massachusetts. They have four children.

Her sister, Ko, lives in Cambridge, Massachusetts.

JEAN and MOU-SIEN TSENG met at National Taiwan Normal University, where both majored in art. While in Taiwan they designed and edited many fine children's books.

They moved to the United States in 1974 and spent several years working in the fields of textile design and film animation before returning to book illustration. Their pictures for such stories as *Seven Chinese Brothers* and *The River Dragon* have been highly praised.

The Tsengs live in Glen Cove, New York.